Tom's Tooth

by Sam Hay

Illustrated by Melanie Sharp

W
FRANKLIN WATTS
LONDON•SYDNEY

Notes on the series

TIDDLERS are structured to provide support for children who are starting to read on their own. The stories may also be used for sharing with children.

Starting to read alone can be daunting. **TIDDLERS** help by listing the words in the book for a check before reading, and by providing visual support and repeating words and phrases. These books will both develop confidence and encourage reading and rereading for pleasure.

If you are reading this book with a child, here are a few suggestions:

1. Make reading fun! Choose a time to read when you and the child are relaxed and have time to share the story.

2. Talk about the story before you start reading. Look at the cover and the blurb. What might the story be about? Why might the child like it?

3. Look also at the list of words below – can the child tackle most of the words? Encourage the child to employ a phonics approach to tackling new words by sounding the words out.

4. Encourage the child to retell the story, using the jumbled picture puzzle.

5. Give praise! Remember that small mistakes need not always be corrected.

Here is a list of the words in this story.

Common words:

a	he	out
and	his	said
as	it	the
at	it's	then
but	my	took
come	not	try
had	off	won't

Other words:

bedtime	jumper	these
brother	loose	Tom
could	shouted	tooth
fairy	sister	waggled
find	teeth	wiggled

Tom had a
loose tooth.

He waggled it.

4

7

"It's out!"
Tom shouted.

But at bedtime, Tom
could not find the tooth.

11

"The tooth fairy won't come," Tom said.

"Try these teeth!"
said his brother.

15

"Try these teeth!"
said his sister.

16

But as he took off
his jumper...

18

"My tooth!"
he shouted.

Puzzle Time

Can you find these
pictures in the story?

Which pages are the
pictures from?

Turn over for answers!

Answers

The pictures come from these pages:

a. pages 8–9

b. pages 4–5

c. pages 16–17

d. pages 6–7

Franklin Watts
First published in Great Britain in 2016 by
The Watts Publishing Group

Copyright (text) © Sam Hay 2016
Copyright (illustration) © Melanie Sharp
2016

The rights of Sam Hay to be identified as the
author and Melanie Sharp to be identified
as the illustrator of this Work have been
asserted in accordance with the Copyright,
Designs and Patents Act, 1988.

Series Editor: Jackie Hamley
Series Advisor: Catherine Glavina
Series Designer: Cathryn Gilbert

A CIP catalogue record for this book is
available from the British Library.

ISBN 978 1 4451 4613 3 (hbk)
ISBN 978 1 4451 4615 7 (pbk)
ISBN 978 1 4451 4614 0 (library ebook)

Printed in China

Franklin Watts
An imprint of
Hachette Children's Group
Part of The Watts Publishing Group
Carmelite House
50 Victoria Embankment
London EC4Y 0DZ

An Hachette UK Company
www.hachette.co.uk

www.franklinwatts.co.uk

FSC
www.fsc.org
MIX
Paper from
responsible sources
FSC® C104740